Rebecca Ladd started her writing journey when she started a personal blog to manage the anxiety issues she was facing at the time until she eventually moved on to writing short stories. She has always had a passion for reading which encouraged her to try writing herself. Rebecca currently lives with her twin sister and their two cats in Essex.

Rebecca Ladd

SCATTERED PERSPECTIVES

AUSTIN MACAULEY PUBLISHERS™

LONDON • CAMBRIDGE • NEW YORK • SHARJAH

A CIP catalogue record for this title is available from the British Library.

ISBN 9781035823352 (Paperback)
ISBN 9781035823369 (ePub e-book)

www.austinmacauley.com

First Published 2024
Austin Macauley Publishers Ltd®
1 Canada Square
Canary Wharf
London
E14 5AA

I would like to thank my sister for inspiring me to write my first short story following her success in writing a novella.

I would also like to thank a friend of mine called Ruben who inspired the man and his robin.

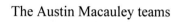The Austin Macauley teams

Table Of Content

A Man and His Robin   11

I Like My Coffee How I Like Everything, Depending on My Mood   25

Midnight Lies   52

A Man and His Robin

Chapter 1

It was a cold, autumn morning, there was morning dew on the grass, leaves falling from the trees and covering the ground in shades of orange and red. A man was slowly waking up from his delightful slumber, he rubbed his eyes, felt a sudden rush of feeling cold so pulled his blanket up over his head to protect himself. He was not yet used to this change in weather, and found himself daydreaming about warmer days.

He was an early riser so he missed waking up to the sun rays sneaking into his bedroom and painting his room with playful shadows. The longer days where he could do the things he enjoyed until late in the evening such as drinking wine or reading a paperback or two. Sometimes he would drink several glasses and end up dancing around the garden to his favourite music like nobody was watching. He also loved nature and was surrounded by it, he could sit in the garden for hours just watching, existing.

If he would allow himself, he could stay under his covers for the entire morning and daydream about summer and the joy it brings him but alas, we all have to leave bed eventually. Time to make some coffee.

It was a very icy morning, so the cold would follow him through every room in the house. The man scurried over to his wardrobe and pulled out his fluffy, warm dressing gown and slid into his equally fluffy and warm slippers before he left his bedroom and made his way to the kitchen.

He lived alone so there would be no possible way for the coffee to already be made up for him. He boiled the kettle, grabbed his favourite mug from the kitchen cupboard and spooned some instant coffee into it. He made sure to add the sugar and only allow the kettle to just about hit boiling point before he switched it off. If you weren't already aware, if you allow the kettle to reach full boil, your beautiful instant coffee would become burnt. No one enjoys burnt coffee now do they, the man muttered to himself. After a quick stir, he added milk and his morning coffee was ready.

He wasn't much of a breakfast person; he much preferred a coffee or two to get the day going. This was for two reasons, one, he wasn't always hungry this early in the morning and two he was lazy and not much of a cook. He made his way into the living room, usually he would make his way to the garden on a warmer day to drink his morning coffee but today he just couldn't stand the cold. Even though he couldn't sit in the garden, he could see it from the living room which helped. It wasn't quite the same but it was almost enough.

The garden was truly beautiful, he was very lucky he could call it his own. Just behind his garden was a forest and because of this there were always plenty of woodland creatures finding their way into his garden and sharing it with him. He loved all animals, but had a love for birds in particular. He believed this was because of the freedom they are seen to have; they can fly anywhere. Not to mention the views they are able to have of the world. He couldn't help but be in absolute awe of them and wished, if he were to be reincarnated, to be a bird.

It appeared to be a quiet morning this morning, not many animals about. This did seem strange to the man, seeing as he was used to the company. The man had been sitting for a while at this point and decided it was time for his next coffee. As he pulled himself up off the sofa, he sought one more glance outside and saw something. He not only saw something, but heard it too. He decided to take a detour and venture outside into the garden before heading to the kitchen to investigate.

He followed the noise, and he landed on his bird bath, where a lone robin was sitting. Being a lover of birds, the man had hoped to see as many birds as possible putting it to good use while he watched. It was eerily quiet that morning and the grass still felt damp under his feet, he really should have changed into proper shoes before going into the garden. He made sure to walk as slowly as he could towards the little robin so as to not scare him away. The closer he got, the robin suddenly registered he was close by and just looked at him. At this point, he would have expected the robin to fly away, or perhaps bring more distance between them. The robin did neither. It was at that moment the man knew, this was not just a robin, it was a new friend.

Chapter 2

The man wasn't quite sure how to approach his new friend, the confidence in this robin was impressive but this made the man feel a little uncertain. The robin still did not look away, and this simply ushered him to move closer. There was a chair nearby, the man decided perhaps he would sit down beside the robin and see what would happen. As the man moved past the robin and found himself sitting down, he was now behind the robin, out of his direct view. The robin turned around to face the man and they stayed like this, for a short while.

It was the robin who broke the comfortable silence they were now sitting in when it chirped at the man. This threw the man a little, it was unexpected and he did not know how to respond. He thought to himself, what would I say to a robin. How could we possibly have some form of conversation without being able to truly understand each other. But as quickly as this thought entered his mind, doubt also crept in. When humans have pets, they communicate with each other and build a relationship somehow. Why should it be any different with this wild robin?

The man decided to say good morning to the robin and with that the robin chirped again. This made the man giggle but then continue with the conversation. One would think it was a very one-sided conversation but the robin did acknowledge the man for a short while and this made him feel less alone than he did when he woke up this morning.

The man chooses to live alone but he doesn't believe he is lonely. He has family and friends who live close enough to visit him every so often but faraway enough for him to feel as if he has his own space and independence. He has never been married or had any children but still has time, if he chooses that path in his future.

Even though he has family and friends, he still finds himself enjoying the company of animals over humans for the most part. He hasn't owned any pets in his lifetime but what would be the need when he shares his time with the woodland animals every day. Amongst those animals are cats, squirrels, birds and on the odd occasion a badger or fox. He hasn't had the same experience with any of these other animals that he has found with the robin. As he ponders this, he glances at the robin once more before taking his leave back into the house. Maybe he will see the robin again tomorrow.

The man works as a self-employed copy editor, this allows him to choose his own working hours and work from the comfort of his own home. He spends the rest of the early afternoon working. Around 3pm he decides to go to the supermarket to grab some food for a late lunch, he hadn't realised how hungry he was until just now. Once he takes a shower, gets himself dressed, he quickly takes a look into the garden from the living room window to see if the robin is still around. He doesn't see the robin to his disappointment and so he grabs his keys making his way to the front door.

The man arrives back from the supermarket and starts to prepare his lunch. He decided to go for a ham and cheese sandwich with mayo and for dessert, a blueberry muffin. While he was eating his sandwich, he had a sudden wave of tiredness so decided to make another coffee. As he popped the kettle on boil, he suddenly heard another chirp close by. The robin had returned, but before he knew it, it had left again. The man continued to prepare his coffee and then made his way back to the living room to finish working.

The next morning the man followed the same routine he had the day before. He eventually got out of bed and went to make his morning coffee. The day didn't feel as cold and icy today, there was more sunshine and less dampness. This meant that he could have his coffee outside, which he did every day in summer.

He was feeling a little more peckish this morning which was unusual. He decided to bring along a pastry with his coffee out into the garden. He made his way over to the chair next to the bird bath, he would be lying if he didn't hope to share his morning coffee with the robin. He felt a strange connection with this robin, the need to share time with it. He waited and waited for a solid thirty minutes, looking around, hoping to spot the robin, but nothing. He wondered how long would be too long to wait on a robin who he had shared a single morning with. He decided to wait at least an hour before going back into the house.

Chapter 3

Over the next few days, he would repeat this routine, make his coffee and then venture into the garden. He would sit on the chair by the bird bath and wait for the robin's return. After about four days he came to the conclusion that maybe he would never see the robin again, and he had to be at peace with that. When he was just about to give up for the final time, he heard a chirp. The robin flew over his head, under his legs and then finally landed on the bird bath and stared at the man, just as he had done the first time. The man couldn't contain his excitement, he had missed this robin and although he did not understand why this was the case, he embraced it.

The man and the robin sat side by side for the rest of the morning, just as they had done the first time. After a short while, without warning the robin landed on the man's arm. The man was in shock at first, but the robin did not appear to be affected at all. The robin chirped away for a few minutes and then suddenly broke into song. The song sounded familiar to the man but he couldn't quite place it. Who was this robin, why did he feel a connection with it, these were the questions replaying in the man's head. This was no ordinary robin and the man felt this, to his very core.

The robin visited the man every day without fail after that day and they shared their mornings together. He would discuss his latest work projects, share his dreams and aspirations, and tell stories. The robin was alert and attentive throughout their conversations and chirped every so often to confirm this to the man. He wondered to himself, how long would this friendship last.

The season of autumn passes by so quickly, before you know it it's winter and winter feels as if it's never ending. Despite this, there are beautiful things about the winter season too. The darkness is peaceful, the crisp cold air is refreshing and sometimes, there is nothing better than being wrapped up in a blanket sitting by the fire with some hot coco. The man pondered these thoughts as he woke up, winter had officially arrived.

As the man prepared his morning coffee, he heard the doorbell ring. This is unusual for a Wednesday as it wasn't post day and he wasn't expecting anyone. He turns the kettle off; he would start the process of making his coffee again after he had answered the door. He opened the door, to his surprise it was his neighbour, Maryanne. He didn't see Maryanne much, and when they did see each other, they simply exchanged pleasantries and moved on. The man was at a loss as to why she would be knocking on his door. He greeted her, she smiled and asked if she could come in. As to not come across as rude he obliged and offered to make her a cup of coffee.

They both sat down on the sofa with their coffee and for the first couple of minutes they sat in silence. This unnerved him and so he decided to ask Maryanne what brought her over. Maryanne simply replied, I'm here to talk about the robin.

The man could not quite understand how Maryanne knew about the robin and why this would be a topic of discussion between them both. Maryanne sensed the unease in the room and decided to explain. The robin is magical, he appears when he senses you need him and will leave as soon as he feels you no longer need him. It is very easy to get attached and reliant on the robin to be there for you always, but it does not work like that. She should know, she had been through the same experience.

The man was listening to Maryanne but not entirely registering what she was saying. He lost his focus and everything around him became a blur. He regained his composure when he heard Maryanne say his name. She went on to say that she understands how crazy this all sounded but it was nothing less than the truth. The man spoke then, "Sorry Maryanne did you say that the robin was magical."

Maryanne smiled and said, "That is correct."

The man apologised to Maryanne and asked her to leave, he needed time to process what she had said. Maryanne left without speaking any further words and lightly closed the front door behind her.

Chapter 4

The man was in shock, he didn't yet know how he felt about what Maryanne had shared. He sat on the sofa in silence without moving for the next hour. Trying to process what he had been told was proving to be difficult, mostly because deep down in his heart he knew he believed her. If anyone else had been told this, he imagined they would probably have laughed and said that Maryanne was insane. He knows logically, what Maryanne was saying would come across as insane but he also knew how he felt when that robin flew into his life. That robin did fly into his life for a reason, he just wasn't aware he needed it to.

Once the man finally removed himself from the sofa, he took himself off to bed with a scotch. After what he had experienced this evening he needed a drink, maybe even the whole bottle. Finishing the bottle of scotch off was easy enough, and before he knew it, he fell into a deep sleep. He woke up startled, rattled from the dream he was having. He isn't one for having nightmares, he even dreams little. The nightmare truly frightened him and he was not sure what it meant. Due to still being highly intoxicated the man fell asleep again, and this time he didn't wake until morning.

In his drunken state, the man had forgotten to pull the blinds before he fell asleep last night. The sun rays were dancing over his face and he woke up in a daze. His head was in pain, it was throbbing at both temples due to the hangover.

The man hadn't drunk that much scotch in a while, the hungover feeling was not entirely new to him but they always made him regret his decision to drink in the first place. He headed straight for the shower, hoping it would wash away yesterday's events from his mind and body.

Once the man had showered, he made his way to the kitchen, as he always did to make his morning coffee. The coffee tasted more bitter this morning, he believed it's possible it was mirroring his mood. The man started to think about what would happen today with his robin, in light of what he had learned yesterday. If this robin was magical, would he know that Maryanne had told him his secret, his purpose. Would he have decided to take his leave earlier than originally planned, leaving the man alone without him for the rest of his life. These thoughts made the man angry and so he gulped down the last drops of his coffee and stormed off into the garden. He and his robin needed to talk.

The weather was icy cold this morning, with a sharpness to it. The sky was grey and the wind was strong. Again, the man was convinced it was mirroring his mood. He walked straight over to the bird bath and stood; he didn't want to sit down. He yelled out to the robin, over and over again beckoning him to show himself. The more the man yelled, the more angry he became and then suddenly without warning he burst into tears and fell to his knees.

The man was kneeling down and crying for at least 30 minutes, he could not control the tears that seemed to want to expel themselves from his body. The man was not known to cry, he had always remained strong when he was upset. He made a conscious effort to never shed a tear, no matter how tough the situation was. This outpour confused him, he could not understand how or why it was happening. He remained there in the garden for a while.

The man had moved himself into a sitting position rather than the kneeling position he had begun with. This was definitely more comfortable and also enabled him to hold himself in his arms and console himself. He had not yet had that person to console him, he always preferred to console himself. The man suddenly thought to himself, was it my preference or did I always push people away to save myself. Did I choose to be alone because loving anything and possibly losing it would be too painful. These thoughts had never occurred to the man before, probably because he was blocking them out by choice.

The man stood back up, wiped his tear-stained face and sat on the chair by the bird bath. He realised in that moment that he was having a revelation, an epiphany. This was what the robin had come to him for, to help him to love something and let it go and to know he would be ok. The robin wanted him to love and allow himself to be loved, he could see this now with such clarity.

The man started to cry again, but this time it was out of joy not pain. His heart felt so full and he was ready to do what the robin wanted him to do. For the first time in his life his heart and his mind were open and he would be eternally grateful to the robin for flying into his life. Maryanne was also in her garden that morning, she had heard the cries of pain and the cries of joy. She knew that the man had finally understood, just as she had all those years ago. The robin would never return here, but he would be fulfilling his purpose all over the world for eternity. This thought made Maryanne smile, and with that she made her way back into her home.

I Like My Coffee How I Like
Everything, Depending
on My Mood

Chapter 1

I woke up today in a foul mood. This was due to being struck away from my lovely, peaceful deep sleep. Not all nights allow deep sleep, so I appreciate them when they occur. Alas, work had other plans. So, if work starts at 9am I need to be up and out the door in 45 minutes, I can totally manage this. I'm actually a very organised person, I like things better when they are planned accordingly. I can't handle being late so even though my mood is foul, I have this all under control.

As I'm en-route to work via public transport, (driving would just give me anxiety) I ponder the thought, I bet almost half these people on the way to work are questioning their life choices. I mean I definitely am. Hi my name is Mel, and I work in an office. I could have introduced myself at the start, but I wanted to dive right in. What type of office worker am I, you might ask? I am an office manager. Totally suits my personality and the need for organisation. Do I enjoy being an office manager? A very good question. Honest answer, I like work how I like everything else, mood depending.

The guy with the red and white spotty tie catches my eye, he looks jolly, he doesn't seem to have the same expression as me and others on this train journey. Maybe he is happy with his life choices, or maybe he is just a professional at hiding his true emotions. I for one currently have a resting bitch face, this is evident for all who dare look at me. I see a ring, so he is married, I reckon he also has a few kids, no evidence to suggest this but I have a feeling. The vibe a person gives off can be very telling, however, do we ever really know anyone? Deep for a Tuesday morning I know. For the rest of the journey, I pull out my paperback, there is nothing I love more than a good ole read, anywhere at any time.

As I edge closer to the building where I work, I get a sudden shudder. This shudder was brought on with the knowledge I am going to have to face my work colleagues. I like my work colleagues but only in small doses, this is challenging considering I have to spend 8 hours with them every weekday. Lorna is the accountant; Mark is the receptionist and Lulu is the intern. Lorna is lovely; however, she loves to gossip and also loves to chit chat about life in general ALL OF THE TIME. Mark is a bit of a twat, he thinks the world revolves around him and lastly, we have Lulu, she is also lovely, but has no real work ethic and floats around the office for the most part.

The first person I have to face is Mark, being the receptionist, he is the face of the company as it were, and he most definitely likes to babble on about this fact. I try to avoid eye contact with Mark, this is clearly rude, but that doesn't stop him. "Morning Mel, good weekend? Mine was great, the strangest thing happened to me…" I cut Mark off with a I'm not in the mood for your shit today glare as I walk past, and he just laughs. He is fully aware of my mood swings and finds them amusing, this works in my favour as he leaves me alone. Guys like Mark require your full attention when they are talking to you about anything, no matter how uninterested you may be. He won't get any enjoyment out of a conversation unless you make him feel like the only man in the world. I take a detour into the kitchen first, to pop my lunch box into the fridge, Lulu floats in, on cue. "Hi Mel, how are you?"

"Lulu as much as I would love to chat, busy day ahead, bye now."

I would have said you know the drill, but as previously mentioned, Lulu does not know the drill, and she never will.

Finally, I'm in my office, my solace, my quiet place. "MELLLLLLLLLLLLL, darling,"

Oh no, it's Lorna. I have asked the boss for a lock; (he did look at me rather strangely when this was suggested) and to my surprise, he said no. No lock means uninvited guests enter my office whenever they want. "Mel, did you hear me?"

Unfortunately, I did hear her. "Hi Lorna, what do I owe this pleasure?"

"Well, I just wanted to check in, see what's happening in Mel's world."

"Lorna, nothing new, sorry to disappoint. I'm super busy today, so can you please give me some space?" "Sure honey, I'll give you the update on my date last weekend at lunchtime. Are you still going at around 12:30pm?"

"Erm, that's the plan, but plans can change. Maybe I'll see you later, have a good day now Lorna."

PEACE AT LAST.

Chapter 2

Home time is the best time, sure I love keeping myself busy and having a purpose but even so, I don't like people that much. Being at home, I am only responsible for entertaining myself, and my two hamsters. I could have gone for a cat but I don't feel as if I want too much responsibility at this point in my young life. I'm not that young, I'm just lazy and selfish. I would ask you to guess my age but I guarantee you'd get it wrong. I am 32, yes, 32 is my age. Moving swiftly on, as I am only cooking for one, microwave meal it is. I don't know why people knock microwave meals, I mean I make sure it's Tesco's finest range or from Marks & Spencer's as to affirm my high standards. As my beef stroganoff is circling in the microwave, I plan my evening ahead. After dinner, tea, and a mince pie, whilst eating said mince pie and drinking said tea, I will watch dinner date on Netflix. Perfect evening.

Here's the 411 on dinner date (whether you care to know or not), it's a dating show (you could've guessed that surely) whereby a singleton, looks at menus cooked by five other singletons, and out of the five presented, three will go on a blind date with the singleton looking at the menus. Decent program to watch to pass the time however, some of the contestants are absolute TWATS. I do sit there for the most part swearing at the TV and trying to understand why these people act the way they do. You want to know why someone is single, just watch them on a dating show.

Coco and Pops my babies also enjoy a bit of dinner date, they run around in their little exercise balls and pause in front of the TV. I mean I can't be sure they are watching the TV but I like to think Coco and Pops are special hamsters who can recognise more than the typical hamster. Or maybe it's just a way to make me feel as if I'm not watching TV all alone. Drink anyone? Just kidding, I am a strong, independent woman who does not need a man. I have my fabulous job, my fabulous 'rented' flat, fabulous friends, you get the idea, I have a FABULOUS life, (sarcasm will get you everywhere). I'll just grab that drink now.

Deep into an episode of dinner date, my phone dings and it is my best friend. My best friend is my mother, I have other friends (that I can count on one hand) but alas, mum is my numero uno. I'm not surprised by this message as mum messages me at the same time, same day every week, just to check in. Mum is under the impression that I have a FABULOUS life but the truth of the matter is, it's simply average. I don't have the heart to tell her this though, I just exaggerate things for her to make her happy and tell a little white lie, maybe five. She'll say things like, "How's work dear?"

And I find myself saying things like, "I had just the best day, I got so much done, had a girly lunch with my work friends, drinks with the team after work." When the reality is, my day was actually mediocre, I got disturbed at lunchtime by Lorna and Lulu, (they ambushed me in Pret and took it upon themselves to share my table) and lastly, everyone else went for drinks while I went home as soon as the clock struck 5:00pm. Mum is satisfied for now, until next week. I wonder how creative I'll have to get, if I continue to lie to my mum, I'll worry about that later.

Chapter 3

I do wonder if people think as much as I do, are people also living inside their head more than they'd like to admit? I am fully aware I live inside my head; acceptance is key to making sure you live life every day as best you can, despite the flaws you feel you and your life have. It's Monday again, like it is every week, whose idea was it to make us work five days a week and rest for two? I feel as if a four-day week and a three-day weekend would be way more appropriate. Alas, I do not rule the world. To start my day the right way, I pop into the coffee shop by the station for a cappuccino, it will always either be a cappuccino or a flat white for me, they hit the spot. I much prefer the specialty coffee places, sure I can enjoy a caramel macchiato and I can also enjoy a pumpkin spiced latte from Starbucks but they don't quite compare. After I finish my coffee, I instantly feel chirpier, the small things in life truly are taken for granted, give me a good cup of coffee or a square of chocolate, I'll be delighted.

Work is quiet, and when work is quiet, I browse social media, discreetly of course. Instagram takes first place, I'm not too interested in other people, I am interested however, in interior design and artwork. I scroll through and save my favourites, after around 10 minutes I move on. Tinder is next, this brings me less joy as swiping through the eligible men these days is painful. No matter how painful it is, I keep swiping don't I? I finally got a match with someone, his name is James, he's in Marketing and he's "a dog person".

The number of guys I match with who are obsessed with a girl they date being a dog person. Why do these things matter so much? How does being a dog person assist anyone in a relationship, it's madness. With this in mind I still organise to meet him because A) it's a night out and B) because I need to put myself out there (need a story to tell mum).

We agreed to meet at All Bar One at Liverpool Street station around 8pm, lucky I dressed smart casual today so my attire is date appropriate. I like All Bar One so if the guy is the worst, at least I can get 2 for 1 cocktail for myself, I will have a good time even if I'm wasted on a first date.

Chapter 4

As if his profile wasn't enough of a slight red flag, he is late. I am a very punctual person so therefore being late is a major red flag. When I'm just about to head home, due to being left standing outside the bar for 20 minutes, as if like magic, James appears. At least he looks like his pictures, catfishing is all the rage these days and luckily, I have not yet been a victim of this. James hurries over and apologises profusely for his lateness, I accept his apology for the two reasons I accepted the date earlier so we head into the bar. We start the general chit chat, small talk, you expect from a first date and it's going alright so far. I am counting the minutes until he brings up the whole dog thing and right on cue, James asks me, "So Mel, are you a cat or dog person?"

And he was doing so well. "I am neither a cat nor a dog person James, I am merely a person who would be happy to own either a dog or a cat. I actually have two hamsters at home."

James stares at me blankly, clearly this is not the answer he was hoping for, I smile and take a sip from my mojito and await a response.

Four Mojitos in and I can confirm I am tipsy. James is rambling on about his work, his friends, and he hasn't asked me a question about myself in the last 30 minutes. I'm ready to call it a night, I'm suddenly craving a Big Mac and cannot stand listening to James any further. "Sorry to interrupt, as lovely as this was, I'm going to head out, take care James."

I don't wait to hear his response; I just haul my ass out of there to McDonald's. The beauty of online dating my dear friends.

Chapter 5

Tuesdays are just as bad as Mondays. However, they are a lot worse with a hangover. Just in case you're interested, the Big Mac was amazing, as well as the 6 nuggets and mozzarella dippers I decided to get along with it. When I drink, I get hungry, real hungry so therefore I unleash my inner pig and munch out. As I'm staring at the computer screen wishing I was at home under my duvet wallowing in self-pity I can't help but feel as if I'm going to scream. This inside scream happens rather regularly for me, it's a problem.

As previously mentioned, my work colleagues are infuriatingly social and they do not take a day off even when I'm hungover. Lorna approaches my desk; she probably notices that I've had my head on the table for the best part of an hour and feels the need to start a dialogue with me. "Hey Mel, rough night?"

All I can muster is a mumble. This dissatisfies her so she decides to lift my head up off the table to get a response. The audacity, who in the hell does she think she is. "Lorna, please do not do that EVER AGAIN. I cannot promise I will not resort to violence."

"Oooo sorry miss stroppy pants, I was just wondering if you'd like a little pick me up, say a smoothie from across the road? It could do wonders for your hangover."

The inside scream that was brewing earlier is now in full swing and I actually audibly scream at Lorna.

Unsurprisingly she is shocked, her mouth is wide open and she just stares at me. Ok maybe that scream was a little over the top, but she brought it upon herself! Lorna leaves my office in silence and I suspect I will not be receiving a smoothie.

Chapter 6

It's finally the end of the day and I assume Lorna told everyone else in the office about my little outburst earlier as no one and I mean no one has entered my office since. The hangover did not improve during the course of the day so therefore the train journey home was horrendous. Every chair I could find I sat down on but due to the commute home being during rush hour I did not get a seat on the train. I ended up leaning, or should I say falling into multiple people and they were not amused. I was in such a state, they were probably close to calling the transport police and informing them of a drunk and disorderly woman on the northern line.

Home at last, the first thing I do is check in on Coco and Pops, "Hello my pretties! How are my babies this evening?"

They squeal in delight; I'm hoping it's delight anyway and I take this as a confirmation that they are fabulous. Whenever I feel like crap, I stand under the shower head for a good 30 minutes. It seems to have done the trick as I now feel as if I could stomach some food. I pull open the fridge and peruse my options; macaroni and cheese, beef hotpot or bread. I go for the bread, toast and butter it is. I do love peanut butter, jam and marmalade but the thought of adding some flavour to my toast makes me feel a tad nauseous.

I don't know what it is but whenever I eat bread, I must have tea afterwards. I know I can't be the only one who feels this way, I would see it as pretty standard. I'm exhausted so I curl up in bed, chuck on an episode of dinner date and fall into a blissful sleep.

Chapter 7

The rest of the week drags but thankfully as the team at work craved attention at all costs I was forgiven for my previous actions on Tuesday. Work was back to normal and I was bombarded constantly, sure this was annoying as hell but when work is dragging distractions are welcome. The team decided to go to a local bar after work on Friday, I politely declined as I did not want a repeat of Tuesday.

On Saturdays I do try to lie in but the body and mind does not always cooperate and I found myself waking up at 7:30am. To pass some time I decided to read the book on my side table. Half an hour later I decided it's time to make some coffee and plan my day. I call around a couple of my friends to see if they'd like to grab some brunch and Hannah is free. Hannah is a friend of mine from college, we don't get to see each other much seeing as she has two children so her hands are full pretty much all of the time. The boys are with their father today so we can grab brunch.

We decided to meet at our regular spot, I see her approaching the table and we embrace. "How the hell are you, Han? It's been a while!"

"Hey Mel, I'm doing great thanks, the boys had their school pantomime last Tuesday and it was the cutest thing, I've recorded it and I took the liberty of making you a copy."

Given this is a very sweet and thoughtful thing to do, I'm not exactly a kid's person. I'm not broody in the slightest but

I do love her little boys. I think I love them way more knowing I can see them as little or as much as I like but they always go back to their mum. "Oh Han, that's super sweet of you, I'll watch it tomorrow."

The rest of the catch-up was lovely and I did miss Hannah. I decided to walk home to get some exercise and walking always gives me time to think and de-stress. I pull out my phone and give mum a call. I love to hear her voice when I'm feeling contemplative as it's reassuring. Mum is doing well; she doesn't seem to have off days and I envy her for this. I told her about the date and how it was unsuccessful and I could hear her sigh down the phone. My mum is traditional and would love nothing more than for me to get married and have children. I don't want to disappoint her but I also have to stay true to myself and I cannot guarantee I will have that conventional life she so craves. We end the call saying we love each other and to catch up soon.

Chapter 8

It's Wednesday and we're having a team meeting. It is brought to our attention that a new person will be joining the company and they will be arriving tomorrow morning. I hope it's a guy, a hot guy who ends up being my dream man and we live happily ever after. Ok maybe not happily ever after as this is real life and not a fairytale but it would be nice to date someone who I didn't meet through tinder. I know people say dating people at work is a bad idea but let's be honest, we're all adults and we spend more time at work than anywhere else. It is extremely likely you will find someone you are attracted to at work and I'm completely down for it.

Today is the day the newbie starts. I'm not trying to find the love of my life but I would really like some male company and if it turns into more, great. Office romances can also be fun, they spice up your life. All the running around in secret, the sexual tension during team meetings, I live for it.

I'm at my desk and that moment has arrived. Mark knocks on my door and introduces Josh. "Hi Mel, this is Josh, he will be the new marketing executive."

Josh is fit, he reminds me of Clark Kent, he has glasses with dark brown curly hair and is a respectable 5'11". Who doesn't fancy Clark Kent? "Hi Josh, it's a pleasure to meet you."

I take his hand in mine and try to give him a strong handshake but due to his attractiveness my hands are clammy.

What a great first impression, damp hands. "Mel, it's great to meet you too. I'm really looking forward to working with you." My knees go weak, lucky I'm sitting down.

Chapter 9

Josh has been working with us for about 3 weeks now. It's lunchtime and I'm sitting in the kitchen eating my tuna Mayo sandwich and Josh sits next to me. He has a cheese and pickle sandwich; this only makes me fancy him more. I love cheese and pickles. "Afternoon Mel, good day so far?" I seem to always become tongue tied around him; this is the case whenever I fancy someone. "Josh, heyyyyyy! It's been great, thanks, how about yours?"

"It's been very productive."

"That's great, I'm so happy for you. Good choice in sandwich filling by the way, I love cheese."

"I love cheese too," Josh replies. With that, I yelp goodbye and scurry to my office. If I don't pull myself together there is no chance of me and Josh having sex once let alone starting a glorious affair.

Whilst daydreaming in my office, I ponder a game plan on how to get Josh into bed. I don't dress badly for work but I could look a whole lot better so I decided I needed to go shopping. I need to get new clothes and maybe if I'm feeling fancy enough a new perfume. If I look sexy enough and smell sexy enough, I'm sure my confidence will skyrocket and Josh will start drooling in my presence. Good plan.

The clock strikes 5pm and I make my way to Oxford Street. I have a little thought about the best place to buy sexy yet sophisticated clothes and Zara comes to mind. Zara is a little bit pricey but I only needed a few statement pieces plus they also do perfume. Killing two birds with one stone sounds good to me. When I think about that phrase it is quite violent isn't it? I do wonder sometimes why we say certain things. I mean let's take nursery rhymes as an example. Rock-a-bye-baby is about a baby falling out of a tree to its death. Humpty Dumpty also falls to his death and ring-a-ring-a-roses is literally about the bubonic plague. I digress.

I found the statement pieces I wish to purchase and now I'm saturating myself in perfume. There are so many choices, they all smell so good. I decided to go for gardenia. After paying for my new things and leaving the store I think to myself dang girl, you're going to look and smell amazing. I was right, investing in a little self-care has given me more confidence and I'm feeling super happy. On the way back to the station to start my journey home I walked past a McDonald's. I turned myself around and thought, while I'm in treat myself mode … I leave with a McChicken sandwich meal and a hot apple pie in hand.

Chapter 10

Today would be the day I would start seducing Josh. I'm totally hoping it doesn't require too much effort on my part. I have a picture in my head of how this will go down. I'll sashay into the office leaving my gorgeous scent along the way, Josh will smell it and then decide to follow the smell. The smell will lead him to my office where I will be sitting on my desk, leaning slightly back and he will just fall apart. He will look me up and down, taking in every inch of my sexy yet sophisticated look and then rush over and kiss me.

This does not happen however. What happens is I walk in; Josh doesn't even bat an eyelid. I get to my office, get in position and wait a whole 10 minutes before I realise, he isn't coming. Rather than seeing this for what it was I made up excuses for his reaction. He is clearly playing hard to get, he knows he would not be able to control himself and since he just started working here, he couldn't risk getting fired. As the day goes on Josh comes into my office three times with work related questions and I behave in the strangest way. I can tell he felt super uncomfortable in my presence and I don't blame him.

The first time he came in he asked me how I was. I responded with, "Better now I've seen you."

Believe me, it only gets worse. The second time he asked me for some paper. I collected the paper from the stationary cupboard and handed it to him while maintaining eye contact.

He tried to take the paper out of my hands but I would not let go of the paper. He gave a final strong tug and managed to take the paper from my clutches. The fact that he visited a third time today was a shock to me. The poor bugger, he must have been absolutely terrified.

Chapter 11

I don't think me and Josh will be starting a glorious affair. We didn't seem to see eye to eye but I think it was mainly because I creeped him out so much, he quit his job and I never saw him again. Luckily Josh hadn't told anyone else at work about my deranged behaviour, if he had that would have been pretty awkward and I would have also had to quit my job and maybe even move to another country.

Alas life goes on and my mediocre life would continue. I will always be an office manager; I will probably always remain single and I doubt I'll be having any children. Bridget Jones reminds me a lot of myself, or maybe the right term is I remind myself a lot of Bridget Jones. To be fair, it all worked out for her in the end, didn't it? Spoiler alert, she ended up marrying the love of her life and having his baby. I do have to remind myself that Bridget Jones is a fictional character but man is she relatable.

Midnight Lies

Chapter 1

Lucy Curtis

There is always that one person who likes to spend most of their time on their own. I prefer my own company to most people's. This is exactly why I chose to take the night shift; I get to be as unsociable as I want and there is also something soothing about the night-time. When it's just me in this empty office I can really process my thoughts and daydream. I work as overnight security for a law firm, of course no one ever comes into the office overnight, but security is needed, nonetheless. The office is on the 17th floor and every night at around midnight I stare out the window hoping to catch a glimpse of anything or anyone below, to numb the boredom. Mostly I'll see foxes or cats rummaging through the trash cans, attacking each-other, but sometimes I'll see people. At this time of night there are certain types of people you'd expect to see, teenagers leaving a party late, people working a night shift like me, or the people who only operate at night.

Those who only operate at night are playing a risky game with their lives, the problem is, they do not feel as if they have any other choice. This reality makes me feel extremely sad but also grateful that I do not have to live a life like that. I have seen some things, things that aren't pleasant and things that you wouldn't want to go through yourself, yet I never intervene. Even if I wanted to, how could I? My job is to watch this office until the morning, I'm no superhero. My shift is almost over, and I can see the sun starting to rise. London is now awake, so it is time for me to go to sleep.

Chapter 2

It had been a long week so far of too much coffee intake and interrupted sleep. Was the interrupted sleep a personal attack on myself for all the potentially bad things I have enabled to happen? Could be. I remind myself that it's not my job to look out for the people I watch, they have chosen their own paths in life and knowingly endanger themselves. Subconsciously, I must feel guilty but when I consciously think about it, I tend to feel nothing. I've been told plenty of times before that I have a heart and soul made of ice and as you can probably tell, this has affected most of my relationships. I'm better on my own and I like to rely on myself rather than other people, other people let you down. It's the final shift of the week so I'm contemplating the weekend whilst staring out the window, as per usual. It's mother's birthday weekend and I'm supposed to join her for lunch on Saturday. My mother has been a single mum for as long as I can remember. My father was never around, and I had no siblings, this is probably why I prefer being on my own and pushing people away. Lost in thought about my insecurities, I spot something outside out of the corner of my eye. I can't quite believe it at first, so I move closer to the window and press my face up against the glass. There is a girl running, she's running naked down the street with blood smeared down her body. No-one seems to be following her at this stage, but no-one seems to be helping her either. I rub my eyes, thinking I must be seeing things and look again, finally I see someone else approaching her from behind. The person approaching her from behind looks as if they are holding a gun, I stare in shock as the scene unfolds in front of me, not being able to move. Before I know it, the bullets enter the poor girl. I hear her piercing shriek so clearly, it's almost as if she's right next to me. Not being able to stomach much more I close my eyes to block everything out, but I hear her shriek again and again until it stops.

After some time, I open my eyes again hoping it's all over and to my surprise they have both vanished from sight. The girl, the killer, the gun, it's all gone. I find myself asking questions like where did they go? How long were my eyes closed for? Was I dreaming? I spend the rest of the shift in a daze, not quite sure what to do or what to think. The sun rises yet again, as it always does, as it always will, but today is different, I feel different. I arrive home a little while later and crawl into bed, unsurprisingly, sleep does not come.

Chapter 3

Sleep did eventually come, ten minutes before my alarm went off. It's crazy how you can be fully asleep, in a deep sleep for all of ten minutes. I jolted awake and could feel my heart racing, must have been dreaming, it's a shame I can't always remember my dreams, but I can still feel the after effects, nonetheless. I lay in bed for what feels like an hour just staring at the ceiling, trying to piece together what happened the night before. After a strong attempt with no success, I get out of bed to make some coffee, lord knows I'll need it today. Today is my birthday lunch with Mum. I have no idea how I'm supposed to focus on anything other than what I saw or thought I saw last night. Mum will be able to tell something is wrong if I'm not careful, she always can. This seems to be a special gift Mums have, they just know when something isn't quite right, usually this is a blessing but today it will feel like a curse. As it's only always been Mum and me, she can read me like a book, she knows the deepest parts of me, this is why I tend to keep the visits to a bare minimum. Today is Mum's day and I am going to try my very best to make sure it's a good one.

I checked my phone for any messages whilst drinking my second cup of filter coffee, knowing Mum, she would have messaged me confirming our lunch date. As expected, Mum asks for confirmation and this is given to her. There wouldn't be any other messages, I don't have many friends who would want to get in touch, no boyfriend either for that matter. I have flings every so often, to feel something. The flings are almost always with unavailable men (some married), as this is the best way to get what I need without the possibility of commitment. Approaching 11am and lunch being with Mum at 2pm, I best start to get myself ready. I pour myself one more cup of coffee and head to the bathroom for a shower.

Chapter 4

My Mum lives an hour and a half away by car, I don't drive so uber it is. I would usually just catch a train to anywhere I want to go but today I cannot face people. As we drive through the city of London I look outside, people are walking their dogs, having brunch, none of these people have any idea what may have happened last night outside my office building. I say may, because I'm not entirely sure anything did happen yet. The three cups of coffee I had this morning for energy seem to have worn off and I feel myself dozing off. It's very dangerous to fall asleep in a stranger's car but I couldn't help it, besides, I'm one of those people who choose not to be afraid of much. I can feel the car slowing down so I wake up, safe and sound outside my mum's house. I decided to tip the driver and give him a four-star rating as the kind gentleman left me to sleep in peace. Uber drivers can either be super talkative or super quiet, very rarely is there an in-between. Today I'm grateful he was one of the quiet ones. As I walk down the path, I see the front door swing open and my mum smiles, but her eyes are full of concern. I've become accustomed to this look of concern but no matter what, I always smile warmly back. "Happy birthday Mum!" I embrace her and feel safe and loved.

"Thank you darling," she responds.

We walk through to the kitchen and Mum pops the kettle on, she then busies herself with chopping up some vegetables.

Mum always tries her very best to get me to eat my fruit and vegetables, they're not my favourite food group but I don't mind eating them to keep her happy. Whilst Mum continues to prepare lunch, I make a start on the tea and not being able to stand the silence any longer I speak first, "So Mum, how's things?" Mum takes a moment to respond.

"Things with me are fine darling, same old business. I did, however, join a new Zumba class the other week, have you ever tried it?"

I answer, "I can't say I have tried it mother, you know me, I'm not really the physical type. I'm glad you've found something new to try, something fun."

The rest of the afternoon is pleasant, after lunch we have some more tea but this time with cake, we chit chat about mundane things and before I know it the day is coming to an end. I have managed to get through today without showing any obvious signs of distress which I am super surprised about. Just when I'm about to leave mum gets that look of concern back and I know that she is debating in her head right now about whether or not she should ask if I'm ok. Here it comes, "Are you ok Lucy? I know you've been acting fine all day, but I can tell something is possibly wrong."

I wait a moment before answering, "Mum, I'm ok, I'm just tired. Work has been very hectic this week."

Mum doesn't look convinced, but she also knows that it's best to trust what I'm saying unless proven otherwise (for her own peace of mind). We embrace again at the door and again, I feel safe and loved. I throw her a little wave and get into my uber, the distressing thoughts resurfacing for the journey home.

Chapter 5

A typical Saturday evening for me would usually be, my favourite takeaway, a bottle of wine and trashy TV. I watch trashy TV because it has no real meaning and you don't need to focus at all to watch it. Tonight however, I can't eat due to the nausea I seem to be experiencing and even though I consider getting something a lot stronger than wine to make myself feel numb, I decide that if I'm going to really figure out what happened that night, I will need a clear head so this should be avoided. I lay down on the sofa and I closed my eyes. I tried to steady my heart rate by breathing in and out slowly and trying to remember that night. I'm staring out the office window, my face pressed up against the glass, I see a figure I believe to be a woman. I see the blood smears, but the image of the woman's face is blurry, I try to close my eyes more tightly, hoping this will make her face clearer to me, it doesn't. I open my eyes, back in the present and sigh, let's try this again. I decided to try and picture the killer and the weapon instead this time. The gun is as clear as day to me but just like the victim, the killer is a blur. How am I supposed to move forward with my life if I cannot remember a damn thing of value about that night. If what happened was real, I was the only person who witnessed it, the only person who may be able to help catch the killer. If what happened was not real, then what did that mean for me? This reality is too scary to fathom, I need a drink.

Two hours and six, maybe ten shots of whiskey later I find myself falling into a comatose like state, I was drunk that was for certain, and my body was shutting down for the rest of the night. Tomorrow was another day, I just hoped and prayed for it to be a better one. Due to passing out last night the curtains have been left open, the morning light shines into the living room and wakes me up. As I open my eyes slowly, the sun burns into them and I find myself squinting, I roll myself over onto my front to shield my eyes away from the sun and I drift off again. I wake up an hour later only to be greeted with an excruciating shooting pain through my head, I need some water and a shower ASAP. Two pints of water and a shower later, I start to feel human again, only slightly. I need to get out of the house, fresh air is desperately needed. I walk for what feels like hours and in my current fragile state, I should really sit down. I find a public bench along the high street and sit myself down. It's surprisingly busy for a Sunday and I would have much preferred it to be quieter. As a force of habit, I people watch, nothing seems to be out of the ordinary today until I glance to my left. I feel a presence, almost like someone or something is watching me. I stare in the same direction, to the left, amongst the crowds of people I see a figure. I don't think I know who this person is, but it feels like they know me, they are staring directly at me, almost through me. Before I can look long enough to see if I recognise them, they vanish, just like the other night. This cannot be a coincidence, but I am hoping deep down that it is, and with that, I start to briskly walk home. I didn't feel safe and based on today's events, I'm not entirely sure I will ever feel safe again.

Chapter 6

Everywhere I go now, the supermarket, work, all I feel is fear. There is somebody watching my every move, I can feel it, it's unsettling to say the least. I sleep with one eye open; I'm always looking behind when I'm walking around. What if I was next? This killer, this thing, knows I saw the murder take place, I don't know how but they have found me. Worse part of all of this is that I haven't even told a soul, this killer is not being chased by the cops, so why follow me around? The only thing I can think of is that this killer doesn't care about what I could do, they just want to kill me next. They say serial killers have a type; I could be the perfect fit for the sick, twisted fantasy this killer needs to satisfy. I think I need to lie down.

After a short nap I decided to turn on the TV to catch up on the news. I don't usually watch the news as I just find it depressing but I am waiting for someone to find the victim, she must be out there somewhere, there must be someone who misses her. This has become a daily habit and just about when I decide to turn the TV off to get ready for my shift, I see it. The victim I witnessed being murdered is finally on the news, she was finally found. She was so pretty, blond hair, green eyes, around 5'3". What a waste, this poor woman who is around only 25 years old, the reporter states, has had her life cut short by a sadistic killer. Whilst I stare at the TV, at this poor woman's picture, I can't help but notice we look similar,

I have blond hair, blue eyes and I'm around 5'1". This turns my blood cold and I freeze, I was the killer's type, as far as I was concerned, I was a dead woman at this point. Today was Thursday, and my shift was about to start shortly. I best get myself ready. I arrive at the office building just within enough time not to be late. I can't help but think I wish it was summer right now, not because I dislike cooler weather, but because it's light outside until 9pm. I used to find the night-time soothing; I now find it terrifying. Bad things only seem to happen at night, this never used to bother me, or cross my mind, until I witnessed a murder.

I walk into the foyer and press the lift button, I'm alone at first but then I feel a presence next to me. I'm too scared to turn and look but it turns out I didn't need to, the person spoke. "Hi Lucy."

It's a voice I don't recognise. I have to turn now, I need to look at this person, I need to see who they are. I turn my head slowly and I see him, the killer, I'm sure of it.

"How do you know my name?" The man waits a moment and then speaks.

"I know all about you Lucy, it's my job to know who my potential victims are."

I don't know what to do and I'm paralysed with fear. After this response, the man leaves and the lift doors open, I step inside alone and press my floor number. I was a dead woman.

Chapter 7

Ever since my encounter with my maker I haven't been eating, sleeping or answering any of my Mums' phone calls. I lay awake wondering; does he know where I live and if so, does he watch me from the outside. He already knows where I work, it isn't much of a stretch to imagine he also knows my personal home address as well. Right now, I am living off of coffee and fear, not the best combination but I cannot eat a damn thing. My days take place in a haze, I get out of bed, shower, get dressed, drink coffee, go to work, come home, repeat. I never walk alone at night anymore, I always make sure I get a cab home, buses are also a little too risky. Yes, this is costing a small fortune, but can you really put a price on personal safety, I don't think so. If I were an optimistic person, I would say something like, oh at least I've lost a few pounds! Luckily, I am not but nevertheless it's true, I've lost around five pounds I would say. I don't think it'll stop there, maybe I'll just wither away so I can no longer be seen by anyone.

Wednesday morning, work was difficult last night. I'm starting to fall in and out of consciousness and for a security guard that is just not acceptable. If I'm not careful or if I don't try to eat or sleep, I don't think I'll have a job for much longer. Sleeping pills could work to aid sleep and the no eating thing, maybe I could try a protein shake. Having said that, maybe losing this job would be a good move and then I can start fresh somewhere else. The killer couldn't possibly follow me halfway around the country just to murder me, that seems like a lot of effort but then again, he lives for killing and I am his prey. I haven't just been ignoring my Mums' calls because I am in a crisis, I do not want her to come to any harm and I have a feeling if we talk, she will know something is wrong and she will want to help. I cannot risk losing my mother, she is all I have in this cruel world. I drop mother a text every so often just so she knows A) I'm alive and B) so she doesn't come over to the house. I need to think about my next steps, I need to decide what road to take and I need to decide quickly.

Chapter 8

It's now Friday morning, a week later and I am in bed contemplating where to go. I was fired at work last night, turns out falling asleep at work has since escalated. I was experiencing night terrors which are definitely inappropriate within a work environment. I mean I knew I was experiencing them at home after I took enough sleeping pills with vodka to fall asleep in the first place. Unfortunately, what I do whilst asleep is not within my control and now I'm unemployed. I haven't been for a walk alone in weeks, but I feel today I need to at least try. I haven't seen the killer since that day by the lift at work, maybe I am at least safe enough to walk in broad daylight outside by myself.

I wrap myself up warm, it's bloody freezing outside. Hair could use a wash but nothing some dry shampoo can't fix until later today. I am almost out the door when I realise, I forgot something, pepper spray. If I'm going to possibly be at risk, I need to at least be prepared for the worse. Pepper spray intact, I lock the front door behind me and start to walk. Breathing in fresh air is one of the most amazing feelings when you've been cooped up inside and the house is in an absolute state. I stand still for just a moment, close my eyes and breathe in and out for about three minutes. The three minutes feels like an eternity and when I open my eyes, I'm still here, safe. With this knowledge I smile to myself and carry on walking towards the local park. I find a bench overlooking the boating lake and decide to sit down. I'm not usually this exhausted from a short walk, but I am a shadow of my normal self at the moment and it shows. I wonder what it's like to be a duck, or a swan. What a peaceful life they live, swimming around, whilst us humans out here are faced with somewhat difficult, or challenging lives. If I believed there was such a thing as reincarnation I would definitely come back as an animal, maybe a dog, or a cat. As I sit lost in my thoughts, the space next to me suddenly becomes occupied and I feel the presence of something, or should I say someone, and they are evil. I knew I shouldn't have left the house. "Hello Lucy, beautiful day, isn't it?" I cannot catch my breath so the silence on my part continues.

"Finally left the house I see; I was wondering how long it would take."

"Leave me alone," is all I can muster.

"Now, if I left you alone, that wouldn't be much fun would it. Don't leave town, or do, but if you do, I'll know. Good day Lucy." And with that, he left.

Chapter 9

David Lewis

I've been watching Lucy for weeks since our first encounter and nothing of interest has happened to my dismay. She is rather boring and stalking her is more of a chore rather than a luxury which it has been with some of my previous victims. Unlike Lucy, I am still employed and had an hour to grab her for a chat before returning back to work. Having a day job is one of the many mundane things I endure to look as if I have a normal life to other people. I work in Marks & Spencer's, stocking shelves, working the till, that sort of thing. I actually met some of my victims here which is probably the only perk. Haven't quite yet decided to marry and have children which would in fairness make me blend in with people more, but I have my reasons. Having a family would be time consuming and I would have to hide my hobbies from them as we would share a household. When I say hobbies, I mean murdering people. Sure, I may read the odd book or do the odd crossword but my main enjoyment in life is to kill. Couldn't really say for certain why I want to kill people, but when I do successfully murder someone, I feel like I have achieved something. I feel very proud and just like all serial killers I collect trophies. Another reason why I cannot share a home with anyone else. To keep it interesting I take a different trophy each time, if the victim is wearing something, I like the look of, say a ring, a bracelet, I'll take that. If that is not available, then a lock of hair will have to do. The lock of hair is not ideal purely because I have a type, the hair colour is always the same but alas, beggars can't be choosers.

I first saw Lucy on a train, and I cannot remember what day, what time or where I was going. Sometimes it can take a long time before I find someone I like, the second time I saw Lucy was when I murdered Marie outside her work building. This was purely accidental; I hadn't yet finished with Marie when I first saw Lucy, so I wasn't following her around just yet. Fate however decided to bring us together again, I almost cried with gratitude when I laid eyes on her that night. Usually, I wait a few months between kills so as to not raise suspicion, but I couldn't let Lucy go, she was early, but she was next.

Chapter 10

Lucy Curtis

He found me, like I always knew he would. I cannot stay locked in my house forever, even if I did, he would get inside somehow, at some point and kill me. I decided to take a trip, just like the killer suggested. I may not be safe wherever I go but I know I cannot stay here; I pack a weekend bag for Cornwall. I have no friends and no family in Cornwall, meaning no-one I know or care about can get wrapped up in this mess. I'm so tired of the fear, if I'm going to go down, I'm going down with a fight. I take one more glance around my house, I decide I cannot be bothered to clean it before I leave so I don't. I order an uber and it's outside in five minutes, I slide into the backseat of the car with my belongings and set on my way. Knowing I cannot leave my mother in the dark I drop her a text letting her know I'm off on a minibreak, she'll be delighted as usually I'm a workaholic and don't make time for anything else. I thought it best to leave out the part where I've become recently unemployed as this would only make her worry. As we get to Liverpool Street station, I can see my train is leaving in twelve minutes, I can't help but wish it was already here as I know the killer could be watching. I see people boarding early anyway so I join them. A packed train full of people seems safer than waiting outside the platform gates so I feel a slight sense of relief. I found my seat number and I am very pleased to find the seat next to me is already occupied, no nasty surprises on who could have been sitting there. I fiddle with my phone for a bit and decide to play candy crush whilst I wait for the train to leave the station. Before I know it, we are moving off.

Chapter 11

David Lewis

"Can all passengers boarding the train to Cornwall at 20:00pm please make their way to platform 22." Unfortunately, Lucy and I will not be sharing the train journey to Cornwall together, as it took me a few days to find the free time needed to locate her. After the meeting in the park, I suddenly became very busy with work and had to cover shifts. This allowed Lucy enough time to figure out a game plan, follow it through and be one step ahead of me. You can imagine my surprise when I scoped out her place an evening or so ago to find it was empty. I know recently Lucy has found it difficult to clean up the house in her current state, but she never would leave the place looking this filthy for too long. Being the clever man I am, I came to the conclusion that she must have left for somewhere else. Breaking into her house and finding a few of her belongings missing did help somewhat as well in figuring this out. I knew she was heading for Cornwall only after I engaged in conversation with her mother who happened to drop by the same time I was leaving, what a stroke of luck. I told her mother that I was a friend of Lucy's who had become concerned for her wellbeing when I hadn't heard from her in a couple days. Being the friendly, fairly naive person she was, she brought up the minibreak to Cornwall. Thank you, Mrs Curtis, you were extremely helpful.

I make my way to the train platform, board the train and find my seat. The ticket was somewhat a last-minute purchase so all of the good seats, as some would say, were already taken. Seat number 35A is right next to the toilet.

Chapter 12

Lucy Curtis

Newquay, Cornwall is a beautiful place, I can imagine it's the kind of place you would choose to settle down, get married and have kids. Not me, I have a serial killer on my tail and I'm not even sure I want to marry or have kids. It's always expected of us to do the normal thing, parents want grandchildren of course. I like to also think maybe just maybe; they don't want us to grow old alone because they love us. As sweet as this is, we cannot predict the future and sometimes things just don't happen for some people. No point dwelling on this any longer, I'll be dead, most probably sooner rather than later.

I wonder how long it took the killer to figure out where I was heading. I left no clues, but he could have seen me leave. I'm pretty certain he watches me every day, I may not see him, but he is there. The Dove Sea Villa B&B overlooks the sea. I didn't use my own name, this is my first rodeo but I'm not an idiot, say hello to Miss Taylor Bennett, my new identity for the foreseeable future. I order room service which includes a double bacon cheeseburger, fries and a large bottle of rose wine. It seems my appetite has somewhat returned, and I am taking full advantage of it. I'm going to eat and drink as much as I can, my freedom may be stolen from me at any minute, maybe I'll order two bottles of wine.

Chapter 13

David Lewis

Arrived in Newquay, Cornwall a few hours ago and managed to find a hostel right near the centre. I don't want to draw attention to myself or my comings and goings so I thought a hostel would suit best. Now, it cannot be that hard to locate where Lucy is staying as Newquay isn't huge and if I were her, I would choose someplace with a beautiful view. I don't blame the girl, if I were about to die, I would probably do the same thing. Not me personally, come to think of it, I have zero sentimentality due to having no emotions. What I should say is, I can understand why someone would want to die somewhere beautiful. According to google, there are five B&B's and two hotels along the seafront. I should start my search as soon as possible. I wonder if Lucy is thinking about me right now, thinking about how I might kill her. My preference is a gun, but maybe I'll switch up my MO just for her, death by strangulation sounds perfect.

Lucy Curtis

Due to the two bottles of wine, I consumed earlier I lapsed into a mini coma which wasn't wise of me. I should try my best to at least keep my wits about me, so I can see him coming. I still have the pepper spray in my bag, I wonder if I should have purchased a gun, I have no real strength, so I won't be able to fight him. Whilst weighing up my options for battle, I stop and think about Mum. My Mum does not deserve to be left in this world alone, just because a sadistic killer chose me to die. Can't think about Mum right now, I will fall apart, and if I fall apart, it will all be over. Knowing the killer, he has already started to look for me, I only have around two hours at most. I get dressed, grab my handbag and leave the B&B; I take the backdoor so the check in lady doesn't see me leave. He will be here soon, but I won't be here waiting for him.

Chapter 14

David Lewis

The night-time is very peaceful don't you find, killing disrupts this peace and that makes it all that much more pleasurable for me. It's quite sad really, looking at all these people in the streets, minding their own business. They have no idea a serial killer is passing them by and unless they are my type, they are safe. My search has taken longer than anticipated but I am closing in on Lucy. I can feel it, with rope in tow, I enter Dove Sea Villa B&B and approach the check in lady. "Hi there, I wonder if you can help me, I'm looking for someone."

I ask the lady, "Sure, do you have a name?"

"The name should be under my girlfriend, Lucy Curtis."

The check in lady looks intensely at her computer screen, after around three minutes she looks up and tells me there is no one staying here under that name. I thank her and leave, the search continues.

Lucy Curtis

I found a spot on the beach to wait for the killer with a hammer in my bag. I've always loved the beach. I know I said I would put up a fight but I'm not really sure I even can anymore. Sensing the end is near, I send my mother a text, just letting her know I love her and that she should definitely visit Cornwall in her near future. I can't come across as too intense or emotional, she will know something is wrong and I do not have the energy to say goodbye to her on the phone.

David Lewis

The beach is nearby, I walk down towards it and to my surprise I see her, I see Lucy. She hasn't seen me yet, maybe I can approach her from behind, that would be the best way to throw the rope around her delicate neck. She is making this too easy; it shouldn't be this easy, but I am too excited to care. Whether she is ready for me or not, she won't win, I will easily overpower her.

Lucy Curtis

He's here, I didn't even need to see him directly to know this. I can feel him whenever he is nearby, I shiver all over. I wrap my hand around the hammer within my bag, ready for his attack. "Hi Lucy, did you miss me?"

Being the arrogant man he was, he didn't see me coming, I threw myself towards him, hitting him across the face with the hammer. The blow to the face knocks him back a little, with this I make a break for it, stumbling along the way. He is on my tail and I suddenly see my life flashing before my eyes, I picture the murder I witnessed but instead this time I see myself as the one dying. He grabs me, I feel a rope around my neck, his embrace is too strong, I can't wriggle free, no, I can't let this happen. Through what must be pure adrenaline I plunge myself forward pulling him down with me. During the fall his grip around the rope has loosened and I try my best to crawl to safety, luckily the hammer is still within reach on the sand, I reach for it again. Laying on my back, I feel him on top of me, wrestling to get the hammer out of my hand, I kick him in the stomach, he topples over and I run. I run until I cannot anymore, I need to find someone, anyone to help me.

I find myself at the police station making a statement of my attack. I was lucky enough that there was a witness at the scene, a man was walking his dog, cliché I know but right now, I am grateful for this. The killer, whom I now know is a man named David Lewis, has been taken into custody and will have a life sentence for attempted murder to look forward to. With what feels like hours later I leave the police station exhausted. As I walk down the Police station steps, my phone rings, it's Mum, this time I answer, "Hi, Mum."